The Story of Ruth

By
Tabitha Dowell

TEACH Services, Inc.
P U B L I S H I N G
www.TEACHServices.com • (800) 367-1844

Copyright © 2019 TEACH Services, Inc.
ISBN-13: 978-1-57258-426-6 (Paperback)
Library of Congress Control Number: 2006927377

Published by

TEACH Services, Inc.
PUBLISHING
www.TEACHServices.com • (800) 367-1844

Contents

Primary Characters

Ahiti . . . . . Field overseer for Boaz

Anphiah . . . Friend of Ruth, who also gleans from Boaz

Aphekah . . . Weaveress for Ruth

Boaz* . . . . . Kinsman of Elimelech

Chilion* . . . Orpah's deceased husband, and son of Naomi

Elimelech* . . Naomi's deceased husband, and father of Mahlon and Chilion

Hattil . . . . . Ruth's friend, who also gleans from Boaz

Heshafru . . . Nearby land owner

Huri . . . . . Caravan owner, with whom Boaz trades

Khentfra . . . Chief scribe for Boaz

Kherak . . . . Ruth's friend, who also gleans from Boaz

Mahlon* . . . Ruth's deceased husband, and son of Naomi

Nahshon . . . Assistant scribe to Khentfra

Naomi* . . . . Mother-in-law of Ruth and Orpah

Nesmaat . . . Messenger for Boaz

Obed* . . . . Son of Ruth and Boaz

Orpah* . . . . Daughter-in-law of Naomi, and sister-in-law of Ruth

Rensetmene . Chief steward of Boaz

Tekamaat . . Ruth's maid

Thamar . . . Ruth's maid

* indicates a Bible character

~ Prologue ~

I am old now, and have enjoyed many years in the land that my mother-in-law, Naomi, first knew. As I grow feeble with age, a burning desire from deep within me grows stronger: the desire to share my story with those who also honor my God, the God who saw me, a young girl in a heathen land, who looked into the future and saw a plan for me, the God who blessed me and made me the great-grandmother of King David. This is my story...

Chapter 1

The wind swept through my hair, as I leaned desperately against the strong trunk of the tree I stood beside. Tears blurred my vision, and I brushed them away with the back of my hand. I still mourned the recent death of my husband, Mahlon. We had been married such a short time when the dreaded disease had snatched both he and his brother from us so suddenly. The sun rose higher over the hills and stretched out over the golden wheat fields, bringing me back to reality. I had no idea how long I'd been standing there; judging by the sun, it must have been a while. This wasn't the first time this had happened, I simply lost track of time and the world around me did not wait. I shook my head and with one last look at the comforting scene, started down the worn dirt path toward my home.

When I got home, I went immediately to my room. The dust from the fields covered my clothing and my face was streaked with tears; it would not do to have anyone see me in this condition. After washing my face and changing into some more suitable clothing, my maid, Thamar, brought me a tray of food. I was surprised at how hungry I was. My grief must have depleted my energy. Exhausted, I lay down and slept.

* * * * *

"Please," Naomi pleaded, "go back to your mother's house, both of you and the Lord will deal kindly with you. May He grant that you will find rest in her house."

I took several steps forward, my lips pressed firmly together. Orpah turned the opposite direction, the odd expression on her face verifying that she too was stubbornly determined.

"We will not leave you," I said tightly. "Nothing keeps us here; this land offers us nothing, so why would we not come with you?"

An awkward silence followed. Glancing back, I saw Naomi sink to the ground, and impulsively I rushed to her side. Tears streamed down her face and sobs racked her thin body. Clasping her in my arms, I realized just how much the loss of her sons Mahlon and Chilion had affected her. With Orpah's help, I carried her off the dusty dirt path to the shade of a nearby tree.

"Just rest a minute," I said soothingly, fighting for control of my own emotions. Orpah dropped to the ground near her and buried her head in her hands. Naomi held out her hand.

"I know," she whispered softly, "I know."

Unshed tears glistened in my own eyes as I joined the two women under the tree. Naomi took my hand; the tears cascaded down her cheeks. "It's alright Ruth," she mouthed. I shook my head, wiping my own eyes.

Chapter 1

A few minutes passed in silence; then Naomi wiped her eyes and turned to us again.

"Please, go home where you can have a life of your own. I can't have any more children; the hand of the Lord has turned against me. You are still young, and could still have a family. Here you have a future. With me..." And the flow of tears started again.

Orpah engulfed Naomi in a huge hug, and kissed her, their tears mingling. I gasped and turned away. My hands automatically clenched at my sides and the thought struck terror to my numbed brain. Orpah was leaving! Once again I fought for control of myself; unshed tears stung my eyelids. Others could come, others could go, but I would remain. My eyes hardened and my mind charged off on a whirlwind of memories. A trembling hand touched my shoulder, startled I flung around to face Orpah.

"Please Ruth," she whispered.

I nodded, my eyes softening. With one last long look at me, she turned away. I could restrain myself no longer and in a moment we were in each others arms. The tears I'd held back so long spilled out. Finally I desperately pulled myself together and with a final squeeze I let go and stepped back, grasping the tree for support. Lifting her hand in farewell, she turned and ran down the path toward home. As I watched her disappearing figure, a sense of unexplainable loyalty filled me.

"Ruth?" I turned in surprise at the sound of Naomi's voice.

The sun was setting; obviously I had been standing here unaware of my surroundings for several hours.

"Ruth?" Naomi said again, lightly touching my arm.

I turned slightly.

"Go home Ruth," Naomi pleaded gently. "Follow Orpah, for she has returned to her home, and her people, and her gods."

I turned sharply around to face her. "I won't!" I declared. "Don't try to make me leave you, I won't." I repeated stubbornly. "Where you lodge, I will lodge; your people will be my people; and your God will be my God."

"Oh Ruth," she replied, taking both my hands in hers, "but what about your mother?"

"I have a mother," I whispered, my voice almost breaking. Our eyes locked. Tears filled her eyes, and she nodded. Involuntarily I sucked in a deep breath and then with a smile I realized I hadn't known I was holding it.

Chapter 2

I folded white linen and placed it in my travel bag. The journey would be long and difficult. I paused and glanced around the room; this was the home I'd shared with Mahlon. I knew I'd miss it.

But life moves on, and I clung desperately to the thought. Since my husband's death, people seemed to think I was strong, almost on the verge of being non-emotional. Perhaps looking at me confirmed their views since I wasn't small, thin and delicate looking. When in front of others, I could manage a brave and determined front; but really I wasn't brave and sure of myself and often had to fight hard to keep control of my emotions.

Thinking back on the decision I had made yesterday, I was glad that I did not regret my sudden determination. Mother wanted to leave for Bethlehem early tomorrow morning and I still had a ton of things to do.

Breaking away from my thoughts, I sheepishly removed my dusty sandals from the bag. Absent-mindedly I had placed the shoes I had to wear tomorrow in my bag, showering my clean linens with dust. I shook my head with a smile.

* * * * *

"Are you sure this is what you want to do?" Naomi asked me for the final time.

We stood on a small hill overlooking the town. For a moment I wavered with indecision, I could feel the tears begin to gather under my eyelids.

'Life moves on...' This thought flashed through my mind. Naomi placed her hand softly on my shoulder. "Yes," I assured her, doing my best to keep my voice steady. "Yes, I'm sure."

* * * * *

"This dust is horrible," I complained, fanning my face with a large leaf.

Naomi nodded. "We're almost there though; just another hour or so and we'll be able to see it."

"This is the farthest I have ever been from home." I commented. "Uh—from Moab, I mean." I said quickly clamping a hand over my mouth.

Naomi laughed, "It's alright Ruth. Moab is still home 'till we get settled here." I nodded my head in agreement, then quickly changed the subject.

"Three days is a long time; how far do you think it really is?" I questioned curiously.

"Over fifty miles." Naomi answered briefly. We walked along quietly for awhile, I could tell she was thinking and kept my questions to myself.

"I think we should go to the market first." Naomi planned aloud, "That way we can get some supplies and then head to my house."

"Your house?" I asked in surprise. "You mean you have a home here?"

She nodded, and I could tell a smile played at the corners of her lips.

"Why did you ever come to Moab?" I demanded.

"There was a famine in Judea," Naomi explained, "I had a family: two little boys and a husband. We had to leave. If we stayed, we would have starved. We hoped the famine would quickly pass, so we didn't sell." She finished simply.

"Naomi!" A woman screamed. I jumped at the sudden noise, and turned to see a woman running toward us.

"Naomi," she cried again, wrapping her arms around her old friend.

The chatter of the market subsided momentarily; that is, it turned from vegetables to us. Within moments a crowd had gathered around us.

"Naomi! Naomi!" they called excitedly, some of the more impatient members nearly shoving to get to the front.

"Don't call me Naomi; call me Mara, for the Almighty has dealt bitterly with me." Naomi paused for a moment, then turned to me. "This is my daughter-in-law, Ruth."

A woman at my left gasped, "What about Mahlon and Chilion?"

"The Lord has taken His own." Naomi replied softly.

I could feel her pain; the tremble in her voice, though so cleverly hidden, had not escaped my notice. I slipped my arm around her.

"It's a pleasure to meet you all," I said mustering courage I didn't feel. "The journey's been long, and Mother's tired; if you'll please excuse us, we'd better hurry home."

The crowd backed away and several nodded understandingly. I lifted the basket of produce we had just bought and guided Naomi away from the crowd.

* * * * *

I pulled the blanket up to my chin, and turned over on my reed mat. Tears spilled down my cheeks, and loneliness engulfed me.

"El Shaddai, my mother's God," I whispered into the darkness; "please heal the hurt the deaths of Mahlon and Chilion bring to us. Protect me in this new land. And give me an unswerving loyalty to Naomi that I never leave her." I squeezed my eyes shut, and fell into a peaceful sleep.

Chapter 3

"The barley harvest has been good this year, Master," Khentfra remarked, handing Boaz a tablet.

"So I see," Boaz replied scanning the tablet with shrewd eyes. "The records show that some of my storehouses are already full and the harvest has hardly begun," he said thoughtfully.

Khentfra ran his finger down a column of the tablet he held, making a black check beside a figure.

"Why do you suppose we have had so much increase this year?" Boaz questioned. "Good weather conditions?"

Khentfra shrugged. "It could be a number of things."

"Hmm," Boaz dropped the tablet on the scribe's table and stood up. "Tell Ahiti that I want to see him about the barley in that storehouse that flooded last year," Boaz instructed, "we don't want to lose that much grain again when the wet weather comes."

The scribe nodded, quickly making a note in the side column. "Anything else, Master?"

"Not at the moment," Boaz replied. "In a few weeks we should begin the work on the new storehouses, but that can wait until after harvest," he continued, studying the scribe intently. "Also, those two fields behind Heshafru's estate will need to be cleared before planting season."

Khentfra nodded absent-mindedly, still writing in some column. Boaz turned to leave, then turned back abruptly. "Remind me when Huri's caravan comes through here again. We need more olive oil and goat skins."

"Yes, Master."

* * * * *

"What kind of field is that?" I asked, jerking my head toward the nearby field to indicate what I was talking about.

"Barley," Naomi replied.

"Do many people grow barley around here?" I persisted, placing a full water jar on the low table.

Naomi nodded. "It is harvest season right now, and the people are busy harvesting bountiful crops of barley and other grains. Caravans frequently come through and we trade our grain for olive oil, animal skins, dyes, and linen." Naomi punched the bread dough and added some more flour. "The men will hire reapers to help gather in the grain. Those who do not have all their grain in before the rainy season comes, will lose a great deal of profit."

Chapter 3

I glanced out the open doorway at the rows of men working their way across the fields. "How long has the harvest season been on?" I asked curiously.

"This is the fifth day." Naomi replied.

"Are all those men hired by the farmers just for harvest?"

Naomi shook her head, "Some of the more wealthy ones have enough servants to bring in the harvest alone; these are kept year round. That field over there," she said pointing a floured finger in the direction of the nearest field, "belongs to Boaz, a near kinsman of mine. Those men in his fields are servants he has year round; he seldom hires harvest helpers and usually makes a large profit. The estate we passed on our way here was his."

My eyes widened in surprise.

Naomi laughed. "The reed mats need to be shaken," she reminded.

I swept the last of the dirt out the door and hung up my broom. A cool breeze flitted through the house and I hummed as I folded the blankets and laid them over the reed mats. Mother had gone to the market since we were running low on supplies, and I busied myself tidying up the little house.

A warning smell from the little brick oven sent me flying to take out the bread. Someone behind me cleared their throat; startled, I turned around.

A young man stood in the doorway, "Forgive me for intruding, Mistress." He said, clearly embarrassed, "my name is Nesmaat. I'm a messenger for Master Boaz. Is this where Naomi, wife of Elimelech, lives?"

I swallowed, then nodded, "Yes, this is where she lives."

The man stepped inside the doorway and made a short bow. He held out his hand and offered me the message. I took the message and with another short bow he disappeared. I watched him leave and then laughed quietly to myself. No one had ever called me 'Mistress' before. I kind of liked that. 'Mistress', I repeated. I laid the message on the table for Mother and tried to remember the man's name, I would have to see if Naomi knew him.

* * * * *

"Do you know who delivered the message?" Naomi asked folding the paper.

"He had black hair," I recalled. "He said his name, but I can't remember it."

"Was he young?" Naomi questioned. I nodded. "His name couldn't have been Nesmaat could it?" She asked eagerly.

"Yes, I think that was it; do you know him?" Naomi smiled. "When I left here, he was just a little boy."

Chapter 3

"I don't mean to change the subject," I said, "but I've noticed that a group of women usually seem to follow the men across the fields, why?"

"It's called gleaning," Naomi explained. "The women pick up the grain that falls, less is wasted that way."

"Sounds reasonable," I admitted.

Naomi stood up. "Tomorrow, I want you to go and glean from Boaz's field. We could use the barley right now."

I looked up in surprise. "But—but—I don't even know him." I stammered.

"That's alright," she smiled placing her hand on my shoulder. "He's a near kinsman of mine and he'll be glad to let you."

I nodded uncertainly; at least it would give me some time to think. The last few days had been so busy and strained with getting settled that I hardly had had time to get everything done, let alone think.

I dropped, exhausted and worried, onto my mat. Since talking with mother that afternoon, I had worried and fretted about meeting Boaz. I had tried to hide my anxiety, but I was sure Mother could tell I was uneasy. The thought of having to meet someone I did not know, entirely alone, and then ask if I could gather barley from his field, terrified me. It seemed to me I may as well have been begging. This is another country, I reminded myself; people here have different customs. To them, gleaning is not begging; I vainly tried to assure myself. If only Mahlon was here, I was sure I'd feel better. At last I drifted off, morning would come soon enough.

Chapter 4

The brisk walk to the field had helped to calm my queasy stomach. Naomi had told me to go straight to the field and talk to the overseer, not to the house to talk to Boaz as I originally feared. I put on a mask of calm assurance and tried to walk with dignity as I approached the workers.

"Could you please tell me where I could find the overseer?" I asked calmly. A young man looked up at me from under bushy eyebrows.

"The overseer?" He questioned.

I nodded.

"Follow me." He said tossing his sharp scythe to the side.

I followed him gratefully. We approached a well where several fields met; a few people lounged on the ground and a man stood beside a small table giving directions to a busy scribe. His feather pen moved rapidly across the tablet.

My escort cleared his throat, and waited a moment.

"Master Ahiti," and he introduced me with a polite bow.

Ahiti nodded his dismissal and turned to me. "What can I do for you, my lady?" He asked.

His manner was friendly and disarming, I took a deep breath. "I came to see if I could glean barley." I said shyly. "I am the daughter-in-law of Naomi, widow of Elimelech. I have been told that we are near kinsmen with the owner of this field."

He nodded, chewing thoughtfully on a weed. "I think that would be fine," he said after a moment of consideration. "What is your name, Lady?"

"Ruth," I replied.

"Well, Mistress Ruth," he smiled, "go and gather what you can."

"Thank you so much," I said gratefully.

He bowed slightly and smiled again. I turned to join the others in the field. "This is the second person who's called me 'Mistress,'" I puzzled. "Either that is just the custom here, or being related to this Boaz is more important than I thought."

Ahiti turned to the scribe, "Nahshon," he said quietly, "note that a young woman, Ruth, came for permission to glean, saying that she is kinsman to Master Boaz. Make sure you give the message to Khentfra tonight."

The scribe nodded and scribbled the message on the margin of his tablet.

* * * * *

This was the third day I had been gathering the barley the reapers dropped. I wiped the sweat from my forehead. Maybe I wouldn't have to glean for the entire harvest season, but Naomi said we needed enough to last until the next harvest. Today was the ninth day of the harvest; I wondered how many of the women I now worked with, would still be here by the end of the entire harvest season.

* * * * *

"Ahiti! Who is that other woman gathering barley?" Boaz inquired.

"Surely Khentfra told you about Mistress Ruth, daughter-in-law of Naomi." Ahiti explained.

"Oh yes," Boaz affirmed, "so that is Ruth?"

"Yes, my lord."

I looked up in surprise to see a man studying me, a thoughtful expression on his face. When he noticed that I had seen him. He smiled.

"Ruth?" He asked.

I blushed and nodded.

"I hear we are near kinsmen," he said, watching me closely.

I gasped. Here I was standing face to face with the one I had worried about meeting and it was so sudden I had no time to plan just what I should say. I stood up straight and made a formal bow.

"If you would rather I glean somewhere else, I—I will, right away," I stammered, grabbing my basket, ready to flee.

His hand touched my arm.

"Wait, wait," he smiled, "don't go to any other fields, these are here for just what you are doing. Go along with the other women gleaning here and take all you need."

"Thank you," I gulped.

"And," he said gently, "if you get thirsty, the well is full of water and the men draw more every noon. Help yourself to what they have drawn. If you need anything, Ahiti will be more than glad to help you."

I nodded gratefully, and started to say how thankful I was, but the words caught in my throat. Slipping to my knees, I almost whispered, "I'm a stranger here; why do you care for me?"

"Because I have heard how faithfully you have cared for your mother-in-law since your husband's death, even when you had to leave your own country," he replied, holding out his hand and helping me up.

"Ahiti!" Boaz said quietly, "Tell the reapers to let some of the grain fall intentionally. And let Ruth come to drink from the water that the men have drawn from the well."

"Yes Master," Ahiti said, "I, uh…"

Boaz raised his eyebrows, watching his overseer intently, "Yes?"

Ahiti cleared his throat, "Well—that is—I had already taken the liberty to allow her to drink from the well, seeing she was your kinsman and all," he finished awkwardly.

Chapter 4

Boaz laughed heartily, "I will leave it to you to see that she gets what she needs; after all, she is my kinsman." He winked.

"All you command of me, that I will do," Ahiti replied with a grin.

Chapter 5

"Master Boaz?" Ahiti paused in the doorway.

"Yes Ahiti," Boaz replied, collecting his thoughts and returning to the present.

"Khentfra told me of your wish to see me concerning the storehouses."

"Ah, yes," Boaz responded.

"I'm sorry it's taken so long for me to get here, the harvest is unusually plentiful this year and supervising the workers over so many fields of barley has been a challenge; the wheat too is almost ripe."

"I see," Boaz commented. "Well, you are here now, and that is what matters most. I wanted to discuss the storehouses that flooded last year during the rainy season. With the extra profits from this year's unusual abundance, we should be able to make up for what we lost last year."

Reaching for a tablet on the low table, he scanned the columns carefully. "This is the total sum of wheat and barley lost due to flooding last year," he said pointing a finger at the figure. "However, if we do not solve the problem of flooding in the storehouses before the rainy season comes, we will not only lose some of this year's profits, we will fall behind even more." Boaz's voice rose in an exaggerated tone.

Ahiti nodded. "Yes something has to be done about those storehouses," he repeated, "something must be done." Fingering the tablet, he stared darkly at the figures.

* * * * *

I watched suspiciously, when for the third time within the hour I caught the men actually being careless. The overseer didn't seem to notice or else he didn't care. I appreciated the extra grain, but the apparent carelessness concerned me, and made me a bit suspicious. Ahiti was attending to other matters today, probably with Master Boaz, I assumed. The assistant overseer was not the kind that immediately put you at ease; he was a nervous, fidgety young man, with dark hair and jet-black eyes. And he was obviously not used to managing everything alone. I laughed as I saw him scurrying toward a worker looking scatter-brained and frazzled.

Anphiah followed my gaze, and joined in the laughter.

"Does he often manage alone?" I asked.

Anphiah shook her head, "Ahiti isn't gone often during harvest season," she replied. "It must have been something awfully important to draw him away." "Harvest season is very important;" she explained, "without it, we do not have goods to trade with caravans for skins, oils, dyes, and linen. Our trade with the outside world depends on the wheat and barley we raise."

Chapter 5

I listened intently. By watching the other women and listening as they talked among themselves, I was able to expand my limited knowledge of this country I now would call home.

* * * * *

"The only solution is to have better drainage systems installed in the storehouses that flooded last year." Ahiti said thoughtfully.

"I agree. Work on newer drainage systems will begin right away; however, you will have to fill the other storehouses first to give me enough time to have the systems completed." Boaz continued. "We can use some of the barley for trading now; when Huri's caravan comes here again we will buy olive oil, goat skins, and maybe some nuts." Boaz shook his head, listing the necessary supplies. "You may go Ahiti. I must talk with my steward now." Boaz said, dismissing the overseer.

"You sent for me, Master?" Rensetmene asked, entering the room and bowing.

"Yes. I want you to inspect the storehouses that flooded last year. Then see to it that work is begun immediately on new drainage systems." Boaz instructed. "This tablet will give you all the information you need, I should think," as he handed a stiff tablet to the steward.

The steward made a low bow and accepted the tablet. Looking it over, he turned back to Boaz. "Huri's caravan has arrived," he stated simply.

"Should I trade barley for the necessary purchases?"

Boaz nodded, thinking deeply. "We need olive oil and goat skins; perhaps you can get a good price for some wine or nuts for the harvest feast, along with the other things we need for household use," he suggested.

Rensetmene nodded.

"Also, when you go to inspect the storehouses, take the assistant scribe with you to help assess the building cost."

"Yes, Master."

Chapter 6

Today was the last day of the barley harvest. Anphiah had informed me that in seven days the wheat harvest would begin.

I sighed. I'd have to talk to Mother and see if we really needed wheat very badly. My job wasn't hard, just very tiring, from trudging behind the reapers from morning to night. I stood up and stretched my back; the constant bending to reach the barley made my back feel as if it would never be straight again. I lifted the water jar to my dry lips, and then leaned back against the base of the well to wait for the signal calling the men back to work.

The other women were grouped in a cluster a few feet away, whispering. Their eyes shone with girlish excitement at the whispered secret; but I was too tired to join them. The signal blasted the air, disrupting the group and we resumed our places behind the men.

The man in front of me was swinging his scythe dangerously and I backed away a little nearly bumping into Kherak. I steadied my tipsy basket and joined her, gathering a little farther behind the others.

"Did you hear?" she asked, a girlish glint dancing in her eyes.

"Hear what?" I asked in surprise.

"That Master Boaz is coming here this afternoon to inspect and approve what is being done with his barley?"

"Is that what all the whispering was about?" I demanded, suddenly understanding.

"Yes," she admitted, "I must confess inspection time is usually quite anticipated around here."

I shook my head in mock reproof.

"You really can't expect much less," she giggled, "with someone so handsome and wealthy and generous..." Kherak chattered on, but I wasn't listening. I had come to look forward to these little encounters with this particular kinsman of mine.

"Ruth!" Kherak suddenly demanded, "I don't believe you are even listening to me!"

"And you're leaving half of what you pick up on the ground!"

"Oh," I muttered, staring down guiltily.

"Just what I thought." Kherak said under her breath. She turned away to hide her smile.

* * * * *

"Are you getting enough, Ruth?" Boaz asked casually as we met at the well. I could hear the other women snicker, but I ignored them.

Chapter 6

"Yes, thank you, Master Boaz." I replied with a smile.

"We're kin, Ruth." He laughed, "Just call me Boaz."

I blushed, feeling a sense of closeness, then paused, not exactly sure how to reply.

"Master Boaz," Ahiti interrupted with a bow. "Oh I'm sorry, Mistress Ruth, I did not see you." He apologized, backing away quickly.

"It's alright, Ahiti." Boaz said bringing his attention to the scribe. "What did you need?"

"Uh, uh, nothing Master, nothing at all," he stuttered. He made a hurried bow and left, tripping over his own feet in his rush.

Boaz laughed heartily and I joined in. "You'll come back for the wheat harvest?" Boaz questioned. "You are welcome to," he added quickly.

"I don't know for sure," I replied quietly, studying my hands. "I'll have to talk to Mother." I raised my eyes and looked into his.

"I'll look forward to hopefully seeing you." He placed his hand on my arm and smiled warmly.

Chapter 7

"It seems strange to not see anyone out in the fields," Naomi commented from her loom. She had taken to weaving while I was at work in the fields.

"I'm glad the barley harvest is over," I said, grabbing at the chance to voice my views.

Naomi laughed, "It couldn't have been that bad, could it?"

"Well maybe not that bad," I admitted.

"I thought so," she added. Her voice held a teasing note.

I glanced at her quickly; she couldn't possibly know—I mean, I hardly knew myself.

"I used to like the harvest when I was young," Naomi recollected distantly. "That's where I met Elimelech; he was so strong and handsome, and gentle..." her eyes grew soft as she recalled the memories. "And I never dreamed he'd even notice me; but even with all those other girls, he chose me."

"Speaking of the harvest," I said, pouring myself a cup of water, "do we need the wheat I could gather from the wheat harvest?"

Naomi nodded, pulling herself back to the present. "The work is hard though—are you sure?"

I nodded this time. "It's not that it is that hard. It does get pretty tiring, but I'm sure that by the time the others are ready, I'll be ready too." I shook my head; there was more than one reason why I wanted to glean in the wheat harvest.

* * * * *

The days flew by and for the first time since Mahlon's death, I was really happy. Anphiah and Kherak visited me several times and were very pleased to find out that I would join them for the wheat harvest. I now had made my first trip to the market alone and Mother was teaching me how to weave.

Anphiah wanted me to visit her, but I was still unfamiliar with the city since most of my time had been in the fields or home and occasionally the market. I found myself missing the little encounters with Boaz more than I liked to admit; and I found it hard to suppress my eagerness to be back in the fields. I told myself that he was just as friendly with everyone else, and that's why all the women liked him. To him I was probably just another relative. But somehow even these thoughts failed to quench my eagerness.

I also missed the companionship of the other women; their readiness to accept me had surprised me from the first. When I first decided

I would come to this land, I had more or less expected cold stares and hostile aloofness.

* * * * *

"As soon as the wheat harvest is finished, I'll see that the men start clearing those fields." Ahiti said slowly. "What do you intend to plant there?"

Boaz drummed his fingers on the table top and thought. "We could probably enlarge our trade a great deal if we planted more wheat," he said thoughtfully. "It would bring a good price on the market since caravans supply much of it."

"Khentfra," he said, turning to face the scribe. "I want you to check into the price of two fields of rye."

"Yes, Master," Khentfra replied lifting his large feather pen to duty.

"That's all for now," Boaz said, and turning back to Ahiti, instructed, "You may go."

"Khentfra," Boaz said, rising from his seat. "I do not want to see anyone else this afternoon."

"Yes, Master."

Boaz shook his head, trying to rid himself of the doubts and worries crowding in. "There's no way to find out," he told himself sternly, "so just forget it. Sometimes the only thing to do is wait; it's just not usually so hard."

Chapter 8

"Looks like everyone is finally getting in the swing of things." I commented.

Kherak nodded, "You'd think that after fourteen days of Barley Harvest, they could pick up their scythes and fall in line."

I laughed, "Men aren't like that."

"Men aren't like anything; they're something all their own," she quipped, joining in my laughter.

"We are, are we?" Boaz's voice spoke up merrily from behind us.

We flung around in startled surprise.

"You don't deny the charge, do you?" I cornered.

"Well now," he replied, his eyes twinkling. "This isn't a court case, so I don't suppose I have to plead my cause. Anyhow, I'd better hurry along. Ahiti is waiting. You can tell me what my sentence is later," he added, hurrying away.

"I didn't see him behind us, did you?" Kherak gasped, still choking on her laughter.

"No, I didn't," I replied, my gaze still following him across the field.

* * * * *

"You like him, don't you?" Anphiah asked as we lingered behind the others to gather the grain that had fallen.

My mouth dropped open. "Yes, I do," I admitted, "but how did you know?"

"I have eyes," she replied with a smile. "Oh you; only you would come up with something like that!" I accused.

"I think the liking is mutual. Really, Ruth, with you around he doesn't even seem to notice the rest of us."

"It's just your imagination." I countered, "He's friendly with everyone!"

Anphiah shook her head, not ready to give up. "He's closely related to you, Ruth; there could be possibilities."

I shrugged, "I don't know, Anphiah, right now I just don't know." Silent questions thrust themselves at me, and my heart pounded. What if Anphiah was right?

* * * * *

We stopped for the noon meal, and I dropped my basket beside the well and quickly took a drink from the jug at my side. Everyday we emptied our baskets into larger ones when we stopped to rest, it made the weight more bearable.

I was quickly adjusting to the customs of this area; though they were different from mine, they

34

often made sense. And I also had to realize that I was in a different country. I brought my mind back to the present and tuned into the conversation around me. The more I listened, the more I learned, and I did not want to appear ignorant. I had to ask enough questions as it was. I smiled ruefully, remembering some of the questions I had asked.

"How long does the Wheat Harvest last?" I asked Hattil, one of the young women I worked with.

She looked at me in surprise. "Ten days," she replied.

"Why is it shorter than the Barley Harvest?"

She shrugged, "could be a number of things, caravans carry a lot, it's not as needed."

I nodded. "What is barley used for?"

"Mostly as feed for horses and other livestock, only the poorer classes use it for human consumption."

I nodded again. I enjoyed these talks since they helped me to better understand this country. It was nice to have people with a ready explanation and a friendly smile.

Hattil reminded me a lot of Orpah. I missed her so much; we had gotten close, almost like sisters. I shook my head to rid myself of homesickness.

Really, I hadn't missed Moab as much as I thought I would. Whenever thoughts of home or Orpah snatched away my happiness, I reminded myself that life moves on. The past was now a memory…a memory that I would always cherish. The signal blasted, cutting through my thoughts. I grabbed my basket and followed Hattil back to the field.

Chapter 9

"That's the last of it," I said, heaving a huge bag of wheat into the little room that served as our storeroom.

"You didn't lift too much, did you?" Naomi asked anxiously.

"I don't think so," I assured her, stretching my back. "It's the bending over that makes it ache."

"Glad it's over?" She asked winding some wool onto a fat wooden spool.

"I don't know," I replied, taking a seat. "I'll miss it."

"You'll miss more than just the wheat, if I'm not mistaken." Her eyes twinkled as she watched me closely.

First Anphiah, now her?

"How did you know?" I exploded.

"I can see it in your eyes." She teased, then sobered quickly. "Ruth, tonight is the night of the Harvest Feast. Boaz will winnow his barley on the threshing floor."

"Harvest Feast? Threshing floor?" I repeated, completely lost.

"At the end of the harvest, when all the wheat and barley has been harvested there is a feast. It is called the Feast of Harvest, more commonly known as the Harvest Feast."

I nodded. "As custom demands, Boaz will sift his barley on the threshing floor tonight." She explained. "When he has sifted his barley and is merry from the feast he will go and lie down at the foot of the pile of sifted barley, and rest until morning."

I gasped, "A man of his position, sleeping in a barn?"

She nodded, "I know it sounds strange to you, but it is the tradition." She paused. "Now, you need to wash and put on a clean linen."

"Why?" I asked dazedly.

"According to the laws and customs of this land, one of my kinsmen must inherit my properties and carry on the family line."

I nodded, this made sense.

"That means he must marry you, as my daughter in law." She stopped again, giving a moment for her words to sink in. "Since Boaz is kin, and the liking seems to be mutual, you must go, and when he is asleep, uncover his feet and lie down. And he will tell you what to do."

"Do I have to?" My voice sounded unnatural and accented with a quiver I couldn't hide, it seemed like such a bold action.

"You must," Naomi pressed, "it is the custom."

"And others," my voice caught, "do they do the same?"

Chapter 9

She nodded. "It is the custom; you must go."

"I will do as you have commanded me," I said shakily. I knew my face had to be white as a sheet.

* * * * *

"Once he's asleep, I need to go in and uncover his feet?" I questioned nervously, making sure I had everything straight.

Naomi nodded. "Then I lie down and wait for him to wake up and see me?"

Naomi nodded again.

"Are you sure?" I asked unsteadily.

"If you do what I've told you, everything will work out." Naomi repeated, she pulled me into her arms and held me for a moment. "This is your opportunity Ruth; your chance to live life again. Don't let it slip." She gave me a squeeze and for a moment I relaxed in the pressure of the embrace. "Go now," she said releasing me, "it's time."

I crept out the door and through the shadows, I was trembling from head to toe. "El Shaddai, please," I begged silently.

* * * * *

I tip-toed softly across the barn toward the threatening black heap. Twice I tripped over something or other; the barn was dark, and it was hard to see. I was breathing hard...I never noticed how loud it sounded before.

39

At last I reached the pile. I sucked in my breath and managed to stifle a scream as I stubbed my toe on some kind of hay fork or something. It clattered lightly to the ground, it's fall muffled by the heap of barley. I stood still for a moment, hardly daring to breathe. Nothing moved, so I placed my hand on the wall and guided myself toward the darker form etched out dimly on the pile. Slipping to my knees, I whispered a prayer, and carefully uncovered his feet. Lowering myself inch by inch I finally relaxed. The barley was actually pretty comfortable. I closed my eyes but not to sleep; I doubted I would get any sleep tonight.

* * * * *

"Is someone over there?" Boaz asked drowsily, sitting up on one elbow.

I had shifted into a more comfortable position and obviously woke him up.

His quick eyes caught sight of me. "Who are you?" He demanded sitting up like a lightning bolt.

"I'm Ruth," I whispered hesitantly. "Please spread your skirt over me, for you are a near kinsman." I was shaking all over now.

"Ruth." He repeated, his voice showed surprise, but he quickly grasped the situation. Peering through the darkness to get a better glimpse of me, he leaned forward. "You don't need to be frightened Ruth," he said softly, "you have shown me more kindness now than you had in the beginning. And you have said the truth, I am a near kinsman."

"But," he paused, a hint of disappointment crept into his voice, "there is a kinsman nearer than I. Stay here tonight, and in the morning I will go and talk with him and if he is not willing to play the part of a kinsman, then I will." He finished softly, but I caught the twinge of hopefulness, of eagerness in his voice. "Don't tell anyone that you were here tonight," he warned, "we need to see how things work out." I nodded, but I wasn't sure if he could see me in the darkness. "When you leave in the morning, I'll give you some barley to take to your mother-in-law," he added, thoughtfully.

"Thank you, Master." I whispered.

Even in the darkness, I could tell his eyes glittered with amusement. "You are welcome, Mistress."

Chapter 10

I fidgeted nervously, scurrying everywhere but hardly getting anything done. I burned the bread and wove for ten minutes before I realized I wasn't even doing it right. I impatiently snipped the wool, trying to undo the messy weave I had created.

Naomi watched me with quiet amusement while she punched the bread dough of the second batch. I didn't see what was so funny.

I dumped the scraps of wool in the garbage, and thumped the heavy spool onto the floor.

I was worried. I wondered what Boaz would say to this man I didn't even know. I hadn't realized how much I'd really fallen in love with him, his sense of humor and boyish grin.

Anphiah's comment that she thought the liking was mutual had come as quite a shock. I shook my head, there wasn't much else to do except wait.

* * * * *

The sun was setting, leaving a tint of orange in the beautiful sky. I still hadn't heard from Boaz.

Naomi slipped her arms around me, drawing me into the embrace. "You have to leave it up to

El Shaddai" she whispered, "He knows what's best."

I nodded slowly, feeling the tears begin to collect under my eyelids. "Since Mahlon's death my life's just been so broken..." My voice trailed off.

"It's from the broken pieces, that He creates the Masterpiece," Naomi said gently.

A whistle sounded on the path and I spun around in startled surprise. Unable to prevent myself, I stepped into the open doorway.

"Lady Ruth," Boaz said, his eyes gazing into mine. Something about his calm assuring smile told me everything was alright. "Would you like to go for a walk?"

My heart pounded with relief and happiness; unable to speak, I could only nod.

He took my hand in his, "We'll be back shortly," he told Mother. I could tell by the smile on her face that she needed no further explanation.

* * * * *

"Rensetmene, tell Tekamaat I want to see her immediately." Boaz commanded.

"Yes, my lord." The steward responded with a low bow. Boaz thumped his fingers impatiently on the table.

"You sent for me, master?" Tekamaat asked, pausing in the entrance.

Chapter 10

"Yes. Yes," Boaz answered shortly. "I want you to see to it that the women's quarters are thoroughly cleaned and fit to receive my bride. I'm assigning you as her personal attendant."

"Yes, Master," the girl replied quietly. She didn't even flicker an eyelid at the unexpected piece of news.

"Also, I'll have more instructions for you as soon as you are done. You may go."

* * * * *

"It's beautiful in here," I breathed in awe, glancing around my new room and touching this and that.

"Master Boaz tried his best to decorate the room with things you would like," a girlish voice volunteered. I turned startled to face a slim, beautiful girl. My maid, I guessed.

"What's your name?" I asked.

"Tekamaat, Mistress."

"A very pretty name," I complimented, sitting down on the edge of the bed. "My name is Ruth. Come sit down, you can tell me all you know about Master Boaz, and this house, and anything else."

She looked at me in surprise; I guessed it was because I mentioned Master Boaz.

But she said calmly, "If you wish, Lady Ruth."

This time I was surprised. I had accustomed myself to 'Mistress,' but 'Lady' was new.

"Now," I said, "tell me all about what happens around here, and how busy everything was before I came. Tell me everything; I want to know it all."

"Oh," the girl replied with a laugh, "Master Boaz nearly made me run my legs off around the estate compound. It was Tekamaat this, and Tekamaat that. He asked me what color was a woman's favorite and when I replied that it depended on the woman, he gave me the most puzzled expression. He asked me a half-dozen other questions that didn't make any sense at all. I scrubbed the room until it shone and then he rushed in and said, "Now, you girls had better get started." And before I could reply, he was gone again. I've never seen him like that before."

"And probably never will again." I finished for her.

"You seem to know him well," she said, looking up with admiring eyes.

"I hope so," I replied dreamily.

Chapter 11

"Tekamaat tells me that you spent a great deal of time getting my room ready." I remarked as we sat together one evening in the garden.

"Yes, I did," he replied, reaching for my hand.

I slipped my hand into his.

"What is your favorite color?" He asked suddenly.

I smiled; my remark must have triggered that.

"I like the colors you did my room in." I hedged.

"Good," he replied satisfied.

My smile lingered as I remembered what Tekamaat had said. "I'm grateful that you spent so much of your limited time on my room, Master," I said, with pretended humbleness.

"Now, now, Mistress, don't take that too far." He grinned, that boyish, impudent grin.

I held up my hands in mock despair. "How can you do this to me?" I begged.

"I'm sorry." He apologized with another grin.

"You are not," I declared.

* * * * *

I had finally persuaded Kherak to come visit me, excusing myself from all responsibility to visit her on the excuse that I would get lost and never find my way home. It was a sorry tale however, when she did visit and quickly pointed out that Tekamaat had lived here all her life, and would gladly accompany me. Finally, after several threats, I promised to visit soon, providing that she came here often.

"I expect I'll see you so–o–o–on," Kherak emphasized, dragging out the word.

We stood by the gate chatting before she left, when Boaz came up.

"Good day, ladies," he called cheerfully. "I'm glad to see that my case was dismissed due to lack of evidence. It was such a relief." He sighed as though a huge burden had rolled off his shoulders.

"Oh, I'm so sorry to inform you," Kherak said, assuming a sympathetic air. "But the case wasn't dismissed for lack of evidence. The judge happened to uncover more information that will be of great value against the defendant. In fact, the evidence is so strong, it is almost certain that the defendant has no option but to plead guilty."

"The sentence will doubtless be quite severe," I added casually.

"The defendant will most likely be sentenced for life to Lady Ruth," Kherak predicted seriously.

"This charge must be more serious than I thought." Boaz grinned, "If you'll excuse me ladies, I must check into this matter immediately." And with a low bow he walked away whistling merrily, and unusually happy for someone facing a life sentence.

Kherak and I doubled up with laughter as soon as he was out of sight.

"I'm so happy for you." Kherak said when we had at last regained control.

"It was El Shaddai." I said simply, "Since I gave Him control of my life, He has lead me."

Kherak was quiet a minute. There was something that closely resembled longing in her eyes.

"I must go," she said glancing up at the sun, "but do come soon, Ruth. I enjoy talking with you so much."

I nodded and opened the gate for her as she left. I would not put off visiting her; El Shaddai seemed to have shown me what He wanted me to do.

Chapter 12

"Run along and find your father now." I instructed, placing my little son on his feet.

"We go to Grandma's today?" he questioned.

"Maybe." I avoided, raising my eyebrows at Tekamaat.

"Me go to Grandma's, me go to Grandma's," the little fellow chanted, as Tekamaat scooped him up.

I turned my attention back to my weaveress, "Aphekah, the weave you have created here is very delicate looking," I complimented her, fingering the fabric thoughtfully. "I think this will sell well on the market. You may purchase the dyes you wanted when Huri's caravan comes back." I consented. "I want to see the finished product before we try to use it for trade."

"Yes, Mistress."

* * * * *

"Mamma, da flower." My little boy said holding out a flower he had just picked.

"Thank you, Obed." I said taking the flower from his chubby little hands.

"Mamma like, Mamma like." He repeated happily as he wandered about the garden in the early twilight.

"He'll be grown before we know it." Boaz remarked softly.

I slipped my hand into his. "Not if he's like you. You never did grow up," I teased.

He grinned, that boyish grin of his. "Whatever you say, Mistress."

Boaz's sense of humor and impudent grin had spiced up my life tremendously, I recollected. How I had managed so long without him, I didn't know.

This thought brought memories of Mother; she now lived in a nice house just down the road. Boaz had insisted on that, and of course I didn't object to having her so close.

My thoughts shifted to Kherak, fun-loving, gentle, Kherak. Over the years we had become closer and closer. Ever since that day at the gate, she had come to know El Shaddai in a closer more personal way. And I quietly thanked Him for using me as a tool to bring her to Him. As for Anpiah and Hattil, I still pray that El Shaddai will use my friendship with them for His glory.

* * * * *

"Well Ruth, do you ever regret all the hard work of that Wheat Harvest?" Boaz asked, pulling me onto his lap.

Chapter 12

"No." I smiled. "Never."

"It is to it that I owe my happiness." He grinned.

"No Boaz, not to it," I contradicted, "to El Shaddai."

~ Epilogue ~

It is here my story ends. In the years that followed, Obed grew up and married, and it was his son, Jesse, who became the father of the great King David. So now I silently attribute my happiness to El Shaddai, who in His great love for me, picked up the broken pieces to create the Masterpiece.

TEACH Services, Inc.
P U B L I S H I N G

We invite you to view the complete
selection of titles we publish at:
www.TEACHServices.com

We encourage you to write us
with your thoughts about this,
or any other book we publish at:
info@TEACHServices.com

TEACH Services' titles may be purchased in
bulk quantities for educational, fund-raising,
business, or promotional use.
bulksales@TEACHServices.com

Finally, if you are interested in seeing
your own book in print, please contact us at:
publishing@TEACHServices.com

We are happy to review your manuscript at no charge.